Come, Meet
RUTH

Come, Meet RUTH

The Story of the Book of Ruth

Kitty Anna Griffiths

Illustrated by "Willy"

ZONDERVAN
PUBLISHING HOUSE
OF THE ZONDERVAN CORPORATION | GRAND RAPIDS, MICHIGAN 49506

Books in the COME, MEET series:

Adam and Eve
Noah
Abraham, the Pioneer
Abraham, God's Friend
Isaac
Jacob, the Grabbing Twin
Jacob, God's Prince
Joseph, God's Dreamer
Joseph, The Grand Vizier
Ruth
Jesus, the Baby
Jesus, the Boy

All the above books are on cassette, as are many other stories, all told by the author with music and sound effects. They are obtainable from "A Visit With Mrs. G.," Box 179, Station J, Toronto, Ontario, Canada.

COME, MEET RUTH
© 1976 by Kitty Anna Griffiths
First Zondervan edition — 1978

Library of Congress Cataloging in Publication Data

Griffiths, Kitty Anna.
    Come, meet Ruth

    (Come, meet series)
    SUMMARY: Retells the story of Ruth which describes her devotion and commitment to God.
    1. Ruth (Biblical character)—Juvenile literature. 2. Bible. O.T.—Biography—Juvenile literature. 3. Bible Stories, English—O.T. Ruth.
[1. Ruth (Biblical character) 2. Bible stories—O.T.] I. Title.
BS580.R8G74   222'.35'09505   78-16723
ISBN 0-310-25261-X

Printed in the United States of America

To my father,
Percy George Coe,
with love

Contents

1

Famine

When David, the shepherd boy of Bethlehem, became the great king of Israel, reporters on the national news got busy.

"Who is David?"

Oh, to be sure, he'd killed a great Philistine giant. And his father was Jesse, a farmer in Bethlehem. And you could have seen his brothers about any day of the week—there were seven of them. But David? "Who is David?" people wanted to know.

And that's when the newsmen got busy on King David's family tree.

Lists of ancestors were dug up. Some people just love digging up ancestors!

But one reporter really took first prize. Not only did this reporter produce King David's family tree, but he also told a lovely story at the same time. It was as if he made us see leaves and blossoms on King David's bare family tree. King David would have loved the story and congratulated the reporter if he'd been around. King David was a great poet and musician himself. How fitting that his family tree came out as a lovely story—in a book of its own.

Well, the story was so good that everybody talked about it and passed it on and told it to each other, because they enjoyed it so much, even the sad bits. And we have that story preserved for us today. It's been sitting in the Bible, just as delightful as ever, for centuries.

To this day parents call their daughters Ruth after the heroine of the story, because she was such a lovely person.

I said, didn't I, that Ruth is the heroine of the story? So she is, but her mother-in-law really holds center stage with her. What a pair of ladies! There are gentlemen in the story as well. Four men in fact. And thereby hangs a tale.

This story began in Bethlehem, "the city of David," a thousand years before the Lord Jesus was born in that same city of Bethlehem.

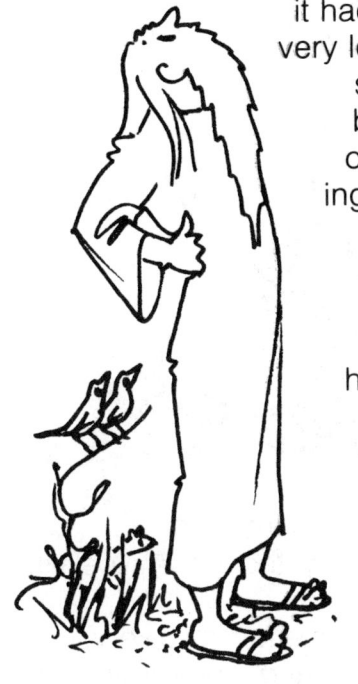

Well, at the time our story starts it hadn't rained in Bethlehem for a very long time, not even a thunder-shower. Elimelech planted his barley and his wheat. Nothing came up! Elimelech kept look-ing up at the sky, hoping to see a cloud. Not a cloud in sight. Just hot, scorching sunshine. And Elimelech had more to think of than sunbathing. He had a family to feed, and if his corn didn't grow, starvation stared them in the face. Elimelech was worried.

He was a good man, Elimelech. (A bit of a worrier at the best of times. Now, of course, he had something to worry about.) Elimelech had had a good upbringing. His parents had been God-fearing. They'd given him his name, Elimelech, which means "My God is King."

Elimelech had a great wife. You'd have liked her! Sweet and merry she was, a friend to everybody. Intel-ligent too. Everybody loved Naomi—that was her name. Naomi means "sweet." An encourager was Naomi. Stronger than her husband Elimelech in some ways. She wasn't a worrier.

"If your husband worries enough for two, why should *you* worry?" she'd say teasingly.

They were fine people, Elimelech and Naomi, and they had two little boys, Mahlon and Chilion. Neither Mahlon nor Chilion was very robust. They were hard to feed, too.

"I wish our boys would eat," Naomi said.

They were all happy in their way, though. A nice little family.

As I said, it hadn't rained in Bethlehem for a very, very long time. Nothing would grow, and since there was drought in all the surrounding districts too, nothing much was to be seen in the shops. Food was getting decidedly scarce. Famine had struck.

Most people said, "Oh, well, things will get better." But a few people like Elimelech said, "This is awful. What's going to happen? Things are bound to get worse and worse. We'll all starve."

Naomi, being the woman she was, tried to cheer him up, but the famine and state of the drought was the topic of conversation every time Elimelech came in from work.

Finally, one evening, Elimelech came in, resolution written all over his face. His movements were decided, purposeful. Naomi guessed that something was up, and it was.

"Pack up!" Elimelech said. "I've quit. We're going!"

"Where to?" Naomi almost dropped the pot she was holding. She had hardly thought it would come to this. "Where to?" she said again.

"Moab! Where else? There's no famine in Moab. I've heard that several families from the area have already gone to Moab.

"We'll just die if we stay here. Come on. We'll be off as soon as you can be ready. Don't take much. We don't need much. One day, we'll come back to Bethlehem, when the famine's over," Elimelech said.

"Oh, I shall miss—"

"Oh, yes, so shall I. But we shall die of starvation here."

Naomi knew that that was the way Elimelech, her husband, saw it. So, being the practical woman she was, she dished up the meager meal she'd prepared and they had their supper. Mahlon and Chilion looked from mother to father, and from father to mother. Their feelings were all mixed up, and they began to cry.

"I don't want to leave my friends," Mahlon said through his tears. "And I love my home."

"Oh, what about my pets, daddy?" Chilion whimpered. "My lamb and my bird."

"We can try to take them with us, Chilion. We must take a few of the goats anyway. They'll be better off in Moab. There's plenty of food there.

"As for friends, Mahlon, you'll find some more friends in Moab. There are friends to be had everywhere. And we'll have a new home. We'll all be together, and we'll have food to eat and no more worries about famine. One day, when the famine's over, we'll all come back."

Poor Elimelech didn't know that neither he nor his boys would ever see Bethlehem again.

15

"Now get ready, all of you, as quick as you can," Elimelech said. So they did.

Naomi knew that her husband's mind was made up. She was thankful to see him positive and purposeful. She hadn't seen him like that for many a day.

She said good-by to her friends—and she had a lot of friends in Bethlehem—and made the best of it.

Friends saw them off. There were tears, of course—good-bys are apt to bring tears. Very dear friends who weren't too busy walked a little way with them. Really, the emigrants were thankful when all the good-bys were said and the four of them—Elimelech, Naomi, and their two boys, Mahlon and Chilion—could go on alone.

Now, the land of Moab, where they were going, was on the other side, on the eastern side, of the Dead Sea—the Salt Sea, as it used to be called. You know, of course, that the Dead Sea, the Salt Sea, is so full of salt and other minerals that you can't sink in its water even if you try. You bob up like a cork.

OBED

BETHLEHEM

DEAD SEA

MOAB

GRAVES OF ELIMELECH, MAHLON, AND CHILION

JUDAH

Not long ago I stood right there on the western shore of the Dead Sea. Wavy lines of salt had dried on the beach. There were no shells. It's very, very salty. I know because I tasted it! It has other bitter mineral tastes too. Someone scooped up a handful of water and swallowed it. I thought he'd never stop spluttering!

No birds flitted around. No trees grew anywhere near the water. No grass, no flowers—just bare, brown rocks marked in places with white, salty streaks. I was told that no fish, or anything else, live in the water. I could believe that all right. I'd tasted it! Very, very salty. Very, very dead. But beautiful, too, in its way.

And as I stood there, looking across the Dead Sea to the mountains of Moab, I thought of that little family, Elimelech and Naomi and Mahlon and Chilion, walking their way around to Moab with their few goats and donkeys and Chilion's pet lamb.

Elimelech and Naomi and their boys had made their journey from Bethlehem to Moab in easy stages. But they got there at last. The green grass and the fertile country made them feel good. There was enough to eat. The boys perked up. There was nice food on the table which even interested them. Elimelech found a home for his family and got himself a job.

Naomi was outgoing and friendly, and soon neighbors began to drop in. They were interested to hear Naomi talk. (She could listen, too!) The Moabite neighbors liked Naomi's stories of life in Bethlehem and tales of her friends there. Naomi could tell a story!

And the boys, Mahlon and Chilion, still not very robust, were growing up, and they brought their friends home for a snack. Their mom was always glad to welcome their friends.

19

Life was pleasant in Moab. They all settled down very happily. Elimelech had his job and was much less edgy, although he'd never be other than a rather anxious kind of person. Yes, life was good.

"I'm so glad we took the plunge and came to Moab," Elimelech would often say.

Then, suddenly, Elimelech *died.*
Just like that.
Naomi was stunned. It was such a shock.
And Mahlon and Chilion were very upset.

Naomi tried to comfort the boys, and in so doing she found comfort herself. "Life must go on," she said to herself and to her friends. "I must look after our boys." And she did.

So life went on again. And soon that happy stage of life came when the boys bring their girl friends home and the girls bring their boyfriends home. And Naomi just loved it when Mahlon and Chilion brought their friends home.

WILLY

Happy days had come once more. But were they going to last?

2

One Thing After Another

After their father's sudden and untimely death, Mahlon and Chilion were even kinder to their mother. The three of them were very close.

Some neighbors wondered, "Will Naomi and her sons think of going back to Bethlehem now that Elimelech is dead?" But the widow and her two sons had no serious thought of going back to their old home in Bethlehem. They'd settled in Moab comfortably enough, and they had friends there.

The nicest thing the boys—they were young men by now—did for their mother was to bring their friends home often. How Naomi loved that! Naomi was a great one for preparing goodies. She was full of fun, and she always had time to lend a listening ear to any teen who wanted to talk.

"Mahlon's and Chilion's mom is just fantastic," their friends would say. "She doesn't make you feel you're wrong and silly when you tell her something. She's got time for you, and it's good talking with her."

Naomi loved having the young people about the house. Quite a few of the friends who came home with Mahlon and Chilion were Jewish, just like they were—a number of Jewish families had settled in Moab from time to time. Other young people who came home with Mahlon and Chilion were Moabites, born and bred. Sisters came with their brothers. Naomi was popular with them all.

One evening when all the young people had gone home after a happy get-together in Naomi's house, Mahlon hung around to talk to his mom alone. He helped her put away the dishes, but he was putting things away in the wrong places. He had something on his mind.

After hemming and hawing a bit and clearing his throat, he said, "Mom, is it all right for an Israelite to marry someone from Moab, really born-and-bred Moab? Is there any law against it?"

Naomi guessed what was coming. She knew; she was not blind! She helped Mahlon out.

"What? Have you fallen in love, Mahlon? Who is she? Do I know her? Has she been to the house with your friends?"

"Yes, mom. Ruth. Her name is Ruth. I know you like her. You talk to her a lot. But she's not an Israelite."

Naomi was smiling. "Mahlon, I'm not at all surprised that you've fallen in love with her. Ruth's a beautiful girl, and her beauty isn't just skin deep either. She has a kind, loving nature too."

"We've had long talks, mom—Ruth and I— about our God," Mahlon said. "In her way she's trying to serve our God. I don't think I'd have thought of her if it wasn't for that. But I was afraid there might be a law against it because she isn't an Israelite."

"About her not being an Israelite, Mahlon— it isn't really the matter of nationality that's important. It's deeper than that. The heart of the matter is what a person believes about our God. Often people of other races have a different idea of God which would be hard to live with. In many cases, disastrous. No, the main thing isn't nationality; it's faith, religion."

"So it's all right with you if I ask Ruth?"

Naomi had put away the last dish. She sat down on a stool, and Mahlon stood leaning against the doorpost now.

"I see nothing at all against it, Mahlon," Naomi said. "We've had a very successful marriage outside our race before now. Your Uncle Salmon—can you remember him? You were quite young when we left the homeland, so perhaps you don't."

"Oh, yes, I do. Uncle Salmon and Aunt Rahab."

"Yes. But you don't know who Aunt Rahab was."

"No, of course not. Children just accept uncles and aunts as they are. Why? Is there a story?"

By now Chilion had come to see what was keeping his mother and brother up late. Chilion was glad he'd come in on a story.

"Well, you know part of the story as well as I do," Naomi said, "but there's a bit I guess you don't know.

"When Joshua led our people against Jericho, the city fell into our hands as the walls fell flat on the seventh day. As our people walked round the city and blew the trumpets, down crashed the walls. Just like that. Except one bit of the wall, where a red cord hung in the window of a house built on that bit of the wall. In that house was a woman who'd hidden Joshua's spies, and she and her family were rewarded. She'd been a woman of sordid reputation, but she put her faith in God, and Uncle Salmon married her."

26

"And she's
your Aunt Rahab,"
Naomi said.
"What?" said Mahlon.
"It's true, Mahlon."
"And I guess that
Uncle Salmon was
one of those spies,"
Chilion said. "Well,
well, well."
"Exciting things
go on in families,
and kids don't get
to hear of them.
I think parents
just assume their kids know," Mahlon said.
"No, not in this case," Naomi said. "I've never told
you till now, and here you are away from anyone who
would have told you. Oh, there was a lot of gossip at the
time. Some of the family were outraged.
"But the marriage has worked well. Aunt Rahab

27

was a Canaanite living in Jericho, and Uncle Salmon was as Israelite as they come.

"The thing was, Aunt Rahab turned to God with all her heart. No half measures. And she gave up her former life entirely. Maybe you'll meet their older son, Boaz, one day. He was growing up into a fine young man when we left Bethlehem—God-fearing and good. He'd be middle-aged by now, I guess. Aunt Rahab's enthusiastic trust in God used to put some of us to shame. She really believed what she said she believed about God."

"Thanks, mom. It's Ruth for me!" Mahlon said.

"And it's Orpah for me!" Chilion added.

"Mom, you're a dear. Your motto is 'our friends are your friends, too.' Thanks a lot. None of our friends has a mom like our mom!" Chilion said, adding, "Good night!"

"Good night, boys!"

Both girls said yes when the boys proposed. And Naomi was really pleased and excited.

willy

When Ruth told her people about Mahlon and took him home for the family to meet him, her mother wasn't very enthusiastic about the match. "He doesn't look very strong, Ruth," she said. "Isn't there a Moabite boy around for you instead?" Her Ruth was so beautiful and so sweet.

"Mother," Ruth said, "I love Mahlon. He isn't very strong, to be sure, but I'd rather have a short life with him than a long one with someone else. You don't know him. There's far more to him than meets the eye. He's told me such a lot about his God, mother. It's Mahlon I want to marry. Don't discourage me, please."

29

So there was no more to be said. But Ruth's mother and father and family were disappointed.

Orpah's family remarked that Chilion didn't look too strong either. But if she knew what she wanted to do, it was okay with them. She could please herself, of course. So she did.

And there were two weddings: Mahlon and Ruth, Chilion and Orpah.

Naomi was on cloud nine. Now she had two daughters as well as two sons.

They all lived together happily. Naomi was an unusually sweet and interesting mother-in-law. The girls, Ruth and Orpah, just loved her.

But only a few months after the weddings, Mahlon and Chilion both became ill. And in no time, they were dead. Both of them.

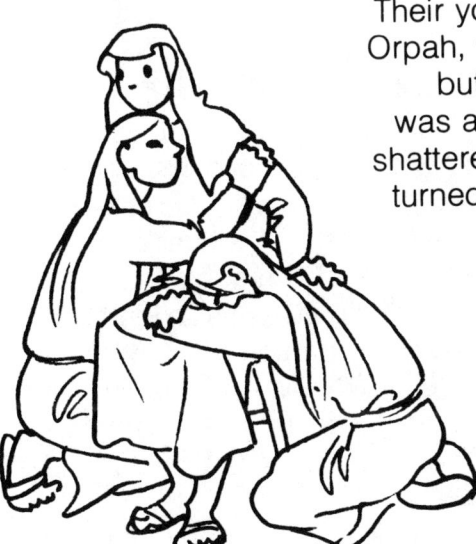

Their young wives, Ruth and Orpah, were broken-hearted, but their mother, Naomi, was absolutely devastated, shattered. Overnight her hair turned white. Her spirit was utterly crushed. She was numb. But being Naomi, she tried to comfort her two sorrowful daughters-in-law.

But all the time God had wonderful things in store. The best was yet to be.

3

"I want to go home"

When Naomi had left Bethlehem in the time of famine ten years before and come to live in Moab, she had come with her husband and her two sons. Now all three of them were dead. Naomi's two lovely daughters-in-law, Ruth and Orpah, had each lost a husband. She, Naomi, had lost a husband and two sons.

Now a deep longing took hold of Naomi, a longing for her own land—Israel—and in particular, Bethlehem.

One day it surfaced. "Girls," Naomi said sadly—and she'd become a very, very sad lady, "I want to go home—back to Bethlehem. I've heard that the famine is over now. I want to go home."

"All right. We'll come with you," Ruth and Orpah said together.

So the three widow ladies set out on their fifty-mile walk to Bethlehem. One middle-aged, white-haired lady, and two beautiful young ladies.

Suddenly, it struck Naomi that she was being very selfish to let her daughters-in-law come with her.

"My dears, it's most unfair of me to let you come with me. I know it's the custom for widowed daughters-in-law to stay in the family of their dead husband and marry a brother of his. But, my dears, I don't have any more sons, and if I were to marry again and have another little son next year, he'd be far too young for either of you to marry. No, it will never do. Go back home, and I hope you'll marry again and enjoy some happiness in your lives.

"I'm sorry this calamity that has hit me so hard has hit you so hard too. You've been so kind and gracious. And I can't thank you enough for all your love to my two dear boys and your love to me. But please, if you want to satisfy me now and give yourselves a chance for happiness—you're too young to settle down to

widowhood—please go back to your own mothers and your own way of life. Please, please do."

Naomi urged them further, and eventually Orpah kissed Naomi once more and tearfully turned back to Moab.

But Ruth hadn't moved. She was still holding Naomi's hand. Naomi tried to persuade her to go also.

"Go on, Ruth, dear. Your sister-in-law is wise and sensible to go back. You go with her. Go back to your people and to your gods."

In answer to this,
Ruth looked straight into
Naomi's eyes and,
holding both her hands
in her own, said, "Oh, don't,
don't tell me to leave you.
Nothing will make me
leave you. I'm coming
with you. Where you
go, I will go; and where
you live I will live. Your
people shall be my
people, and your God
shall be my God.
Where you die,
I will die, and there
I will be buried.
If anything but death
parts you and me,
may God punish me
severely. Nothing but
death shall part us.
Don't, don't ask me to go."

Naomi didn't argue any more. She couldn't argue with that, could she? She was speechless. Looks meant something, though. Her eyes said a great big "thank you" to Ruth, and in her heart Naomi thanked God for this wonderful daughter-in-law.

Well, of course, Naomi and Ruth were greater friends than ever after that.

What a companion God had given Naomi! A beautiful, steadfast daughter-in-law. And all the love that Naomi had in the world—all that she'd had for her boys and her husband—she showered on Ruth, her daughter-in-law.

So Naomi and Ruth set out again for Bethlehem. Two women walking alone. One, a middle-aged, sad lady with prematurely white hair; the other, young and very beautiful.

Ten years ago, Naomi had traveled this same road in the opposite direction with her husband, Elimelech, and their two boys. Ruth listened patiently to Naomi's reminiscences of the journey out, as they traveled the same road back to Bethlehem. It was only natural that memories would flood back to Naomi. What Elimelech

had said as they passed this spot. What the boys, Mahlon and Chilion, did here. How they'd all camped for the night at this place. Oh, dear!

But Ruth was kind to Naomi and listened with interest. After all, Naomi's folks were her folks too. And Ruth liked to hear what they'd said and done on the journey out to Moab.

Naomi, the sweet, pleasant, once-happy woman, had suffered a severe blow.

After days and days of weary traveling, Naomi and Ruth finally reached Bethlehem. It was just the beginning of barley harvest. The wheat would be ready for reaping later. But the barley harvest had begun. The reapers were busy with their sickles in the fields on either side of the road. The barley had a rather sharp, prickly smell. The birds were singing, and there were poppies and daisies and pretty blue flowers blooming all along the sides of the road.

"What are those women doing in the field behind the reapers?" Ruth asked Naomi.

"Oh, they're picking up the dropped barley that the reapers have missed. We have a law in Israel that poor people and widows like us may walk behind the reapers and keep what they can pick up—it's called gleaning."

But Naomi was really taken up with landmarks, sights and sounds of her girlhood days. She remembered her wedding day. Poor Naomi was having a time of it as she came to her hometown that day after being away ten years. Each familiar sight brought a fresh burst of grief.

Ruth, not much more than a teen-ager herself, was so patient and so kind. She felt sure that these bursts of grief would heal Naomi's broken heart presently. Let her get all the grief out of her system, have some good cries, and her wonderful mother-in-law would settle down to life again—thinking of others once more.

The first few days back in Bethlehem were the hardest for Naomi, and for Ruth, too, no doubt.

They did have a place to stay. Naomi's old friends were so kind and helpful. And there was a place that she owned, as well as a piece of land. She'd have to see about selling that some time.

Yes, neighbors were kind. They brought lots of little presents of food. But the story had to be told over and over and over, each time with sorrow and floods of grief. Tears stood in everybody's eyes as they listened.

In the street, too, when the two widows went to do their shopping, you'd hear, "No! It can't be. Never that! Can't be Naomi. That old, white-haired woman! Who's that beautiful girl with her? Whoever is *she* anyway?"

People would pass Naomi in the street—staring. They couldn't help it. Then they'd come back. "It's never Naomi, is it?"

"Yes, it is. But call me 'Marah' now—'Bitter.' God has dealt bitterly with me." Then out came the story.

Was Ruth surprised to hear God blamed like that? God meant a lot to Ruth. She'd left her land and her own family to serve God in Israel. She'd thought He was worth following.

Her mother-in-law had taught her wonderful things about God. However, mother-in-law wasn't quite herself, allowing all this grief to hang about her.

The hardest thing for Naomi was to meet her own girlhood friends, now with their strong grown-up sons and daughters and their pretty little grandchildren.

But Ruth was determined to love Naomi out of her sorrow and bitterness. And she did. You'll hardly believe it, but Naomi became the happiest and most honored lady in Bethlehem. And Ruth? Well, wait till you hear what happened to Ruth!

4

Barley Harvest

Ruth and Naomi had been in Bethlehem now a little while—several days. Barley harvest was just beginning when they'd arrived, but now it was in full swing. Neighbors had been awfully kind, bringing presents of food, but Ruth felt this couldn't and shouldn't go on.

So she said, "Naomi, dear, our neighbors have been so good and kind to us, bringing us gifts of food, but we can't go on like this. You know, I'd really like to go out and glean in the fields, if you wouldn't mind. It would help the food situation. You did say

it was a custom that anybody may glean behind the reapers. Well, I'd like to go, if you don't mind."

"Oh, dear!" wailed Naomi, "I don't know what my poor husband would think of his family having to glean. Poor people used to glean in his fields. But there, we have to face it. We are poor, and we are widows, and as you say, we've got to have food.

"Oh, do forgive me, Ruth, for being such an old misery. I'll try to cheer up a bit for your sake, dear. I'll try.

"Yes, Ruth, do go and glean if you like, dear. It'll be nice for you to get out with the young girls who'll be gleaning too, and I'll have our supper ready for you when you come home. My day will have a purpose now. All day I'll look forward to your coming home."

It was the best thing that
could have happened.
Ruth set out early next
morning with her shawl thrown
round her shoulders.
Which field should she
glean in? It didn't
matter much—they
were all owned by strangers.
It was all the same really.
She was just a poor
foreign widow, an utter
nobody. No family to
protect her. Only a
sad old mother-in-law,
alone in the world.
Reapers were
busy in the barley fields
on both sides of the
road. As she walked and
wondered which field to glean,
Ruth said to herself, "Oh, here's a happy lot of reapers.
They seem kind. I'll go in here."

The reapers plied their sickles, whistling, humming, and singing a bit. The birds sang overhead, and the smell of the new-mown barley did Ruth's young spirit good. Some women and girls were already gleaning behind the reapers. Patient little donkeys were carrying the barley to the threshing floor, where it would be winnowed later.

The farm manager was there, and Ruth asked him if she might join the gleaners. He spoke kindly and asked who she was. When she told him, he seemed to have heard of her and said, "Go right ahead, dear."

So Ruth began picking up the missed ears of barley and putting them into her shawl. She would store up and describe every detail to Naomi at suppertime. She hadn't been away from Naomi for a whole day for weeks, even months.

The girl gleaning next to Ruth was friendly and chatty. The sun rose higher, and the morning wore on. Then Ruth was startled for a moment.

"The Lord be with you, friends!" A hearty, cheery voice rang out across the field.

In chorus, the reapers called back, "God bless you, sir!"

"Oh, that's Boaz, the boss," the girl told Ruth. "He lives in Bethlehem, and he comes every day to see how things are in his fields. He's ever so kind and rich. He's a very good man."

Already Ruth had felt happy being with these people, but she especially loved those greetings, "God be with you, friends!" "God bless you, sir!" She'd tell Naomi that.

Everybody was getting on with their work again, and the boss was talking to his farm manager.

"Who's that girl there among the reapers? I don't know her, do I?" Boaz asked.

"No, sir. She's only come this morning. She's the girl who came back from Moab with Naomi. You haven't heard the story, sir?"

"So that's her."

"Yes, sir. She came and asked if she could glean, and I couldn't say no to her. She's no trouble, sir—works all the time. No larkin' about with the fellows. She ain't that sort. She don't disturb nobody, sir. In fact, apart from a little rest over there in the shade, she's been at it gleaning ever since early morning."

Now Boaz was striding over the field toward Ruth. "Surely he's not coming to talk to me!" She looked behind her. No one behind. He must be coming to talk to her. Ruth did feel shy of rich Boaz.

"I'm glad that you've come to glean in my fields, my child," he said. "Keep coming to my fields. Don't go off and glean in anybody else's field. We'll look after you here. Stay beside my women workers. I'll tell the young fellows not to molest you or tease you. When you're thirsty—barley harvesting is thirsty work—just help yourself to a drink of water from the waterpots over there under the oak trees."

"You are so kind to me," Ruth said shyly. "I don't know how you can be so kind to me when I'm only a foreigner here. I don't even look like your people."

"Yes, I know well enough who you are. I happen to know about your great kindness to your mother-in-law since your husband's death. I know that you've left your own mother and father back in the land of Moab and have come to live among strangers in order to be a companion and comforter to poor, lonely Naomi. May the God you've come to trust in bless you for it!"

At midday, all the reapers stopped work and went to sit down in the shade—there were several lovely spreading oak trees in the corner of the field. Boaz, the boss, sat down with them. Ruth kept on with her gleaning. A very graceful young lady she looked out there in the field, stooping to pick up the fallen barley. There she was, gleaning all alone.

The reapers were hungry. They wiped their dripping brows. Chatter had subsided somewhat for the time

48

being. They were weary. They were glad to sit down under the shady oak trees. They picked the barley heads, like raspy little whiskers, off their bare hands, off their clothes, off their arms and legs. They were hot and dusty. A drink of water first!

Boaz, the boss, was calling, "Come here, lass. Time to eat!"

Was Boaz calling her? Ruth looked round. She was the only one left out in the field.

"Come on!" he called. And as she looked toward him, he beckoned her with a great sweep of his strong, brown arm.

Ruth walked across the field gracefully. How sweet she looked in her plain widow's garment.

The reapers were eating by now. "Whew! She's a beauty," several fellows whistled.

"Come off it," Boaz said. "Leave her alone. Don't let me see any of you fellows frightening her," he said. (Ruth couldn't hear him.)

"Come on, lass," he said as she arrived. "Sit down here with us. Have a drink of water." And Boaz himself passed the food to her—parched corn and bread to dip in the sour wine.

Ruth was overcome with gratitude.

She just couldn't eat all the good food Boaz pressed on her. But Ruth thought of dear Naomi at home, and she made up a wee parcel and covered it with lovely, big, green oak leaves to keep it fresh, ready to take home to Naomi.

All the harvesters rested in the shade for a while after their meal. Those barley whiskers were so scratchy. Everyone was pulling away at them. They're hard to get off you—like little saws. (I picked some barley in Bethlehem just the other day—it was the beginning of barley harvest. There's a good chance I was even in Boaz's field.)

After the noon break, Ruth was the first to get up to carry on with her gleaning. As she walked over to her spot in the field, Boaz said to his reapers (Ruth couldn't hear him, of course), "Boys, drop handfuls of barley on purpose for her when she's gleaning near you, so she'll have lots to take home. A great girl that! She's so good to her mother-in-law, and she's put her faith in Jehovah."

They all got back to work until quitting time. Then the gleaners knocked out their grain in the field ready for taking home. Ruth beat out her gleanings. It came to a whole bushel!

Ruth carried it home in her shawl. Naomi was waiting for her.

"Oh, I missed you, Ruth. Supper's ready, and there's water ready for you to wash. Tidy up, dear, and we'll talk at supper.

"Oh, wherever did you get all this barley? And what's in this?" as Ruth handed her the little parcel of food done up in oak leaves.

That suppertime ended up being the first happy meal they'd had for many a long day.

Naomi was full of questions. "Where did you go? Who did you see?"

Ruth told Naomi everything—especially about the kind boss.

"Let me see. What was his name again? B-- Bo-- the girl gleaning next to me said his name once. Oh, dear! Bo--- something, the boss, she said."

"You don't mean Boaz?" Naomi asked.

"Yes, that's right," Ruth said.

"Boaz? Did you say Boaz? You got into *his* field?" Naomi couldn't believe it. "He's our rich relation. God guided you today, Ruth dear—and no mistake."

"I'm going there again tomorrow. I'm not to go anywhere else."

"Who said?"

"He did!"

5

Matchmaking

Bethlehem at the beginning of barley harvest! The weather was just lovely in the early summertime that year when Naomi and Ruth came back from Moab.

Everyone was so glad the famine was over. The crops were good in Bethlehem and the surrounding districts. Produce of all kinds was plentiful once more in the markets. The country was full of thankful people. It was a joy to be with them.

If you'd been there any early morning during that barley harvest, you'd have seen Ruth make her way out of Bethlehem a little way towards the harvest fields. And you'd have seen her turn in to the barley fields belonging to Boaz and begin to glean behind the reapers who were already busy with their sickles.

Later on in the morning, if you'd
been near the field,
you'd have seen
Boaz, the rich
farmer of
Bethlehem,
known by all—
yes, you'd have
seen him stride into
his barley fields with
a ringing, hearty, "God
be with you, friends!"

And you'd have heard the chorus back from the reapers, "God bless you, sir!" Some farmer, that one! Greeting his workers like that!

Now, if you'd been near enough to Boaz, you'd have seen his eyes search the field and stop, satisfied, when they lighted on one of the gleaners. Then, after having a short consultation with his farm manager, you'd have seen him, the boss, Boaz, the most eligible bachelor in Bethlehem, walk over to the singled-out gleaner who was Ruth.

No, you weren't near enough to see her eyes when he came into the field. But you are near enough now to see her blush shyly as he comes over to talk to her.

"Barley harvest will soon be finished,
my dear," he said. "You glean in
my fields through wheat harvest
too. We will soon be starting
on the wheat."
Always he came to talk to
her—always kind, always
helpful. The sort of man
you could trust
your life with.

These days,
Naomi just
couldn't wait for
Ruth to get
home each
evening.

She always had a cool bath and a nice meal ready for Ruth. Naomi was cheering up again. Did we call her "poor old Naomi"? She'd only been behaving "old" because she'd been so sad. She was certainly coming back to her real self now.

From the moment that evening when Naomi heard Ruth's reports of her first gleaning day in Boaz's barley field, Naomi had scented a romance. She felt sure that on her part there was a little plotting to be done, but she wouldn't mention that too soon.

In Naomi's mind the match was as good as made. She thought of little else while Ruth was out all day. And each evening she'd say, "And what did he say to you today, dear?" And Ruth naturally took a delight in telling Naomi every detail of the happenings in the harvest field.

What Ruth did know in her heart was that she really cared for Boaz. But he was old enough to be her father. He'd never think about her, a poor little widow from Moab.

Well, the very last bit of Boaz's wheat would be reaped tomorrow. Barley harvest was already past. And every year at the end of harvest, each farmer gave a party for his reapers and their families. Some farmers joined together to give their workers a party.

I've heard country people talk about the harvest home festivals of years ago. The roasts and the home brews, and the great barn lit by candles, and the trestle tables simply groaning with good things to eat and drink. And the great harvest moon hanging in the sky.

Some occasions those were! Very joyful. All the harvest was safely gathered in before the winter storms. Food for man and beast was laid by. Good reason for a thanksgiving party on any farm. Every villager looked forward to harvest home. Children always loved harvest home: hide-and-seek . . . jumping in the golden corn heaps.

Well, Boaz was going to have some kind of a harvest home down at his threshing floor, and it was going to be tomorrow night.

Now Naomi wasn't going to the party, but she knew from customs of her younger days just what went on. She knew, for instance, that after it was over, Boaz would stay all night at the threshing floor to guard his heaps of grain.

Naomi's plan was ready. "Ruth, tomorrow come home early, and I'll help you dress for the threshing floor 'do' tomorrow night. You know, Ruth, I've been thinking for some time now—yes, I've been thinking it's high time I try to find a husband for you, so you can be happily married again. You're so young and beautiful, and kind and true—"

"Oh, mother!" Ruth said. But into Ruth's mind came a picture of Boaz—strong, kind, and caring.

To tell you the truth, that picture had been in Ruth's mind at least a few times before. But Boaz was the boss and rich and influential, and she—well, she was a poor, foreign, penniless widow. He'd been very kind, of course, but he'd never think of her in that way, would he?

Ruth was daydreaming again about Boaz. It was so easy to slip into a daydream these days.

"It's Boaz," Naomi was saying. "It's Boaz I have in mind for you."

Ruth almost jumped. It was as if her own thoughts had spoken.

"Listen, Ruth, I'll tell you what to do. . . .

(And maybe, the customs of the day
in Israel being what they were,
Ann Landers or Dear
Abby would have given
Ruth the very same
advice. Anyway,
mother-in-law Naomi's
book of etiquette
prescribed this
course of action.
And didn't it
pay off!)

60

Next evening when Ruth came home, Naomi had everything ready. A cool bath. Her nicest dress. She'd even hunted up some perfume and heirloom jewelry that hadn't seen daylight since former happy days. Ruth looked very lovely.

"Ruth," Naomi said, "I've told you something about family customs and laws of inheritance here in Israel, about nearest kinsmen, and so on. Well, there's a law that says widows like you and me can legally ask our nearest kinsman to buy our dead husband's property and so keep the inheritance in the family. It's called 'redeeming the inheritance.' We, the widows, would go along with the property. It's not as complicated as it sounds. The results are good. The family inheritance is kept intact, and there's a home for the poor widow— and often a very happy marriage.

"Now, Boaz needs a wife. He's been a bachelor long enough. And I have reason to think he's very fond of you." Ruth was blushing again. She smiled.

"When everyone has gone home from the threshing floor tonight and Boaz is there alone, go and ask him to marry you."

"Oh, mother!"

"He'll understand all the inheritance bit. You just do as I say, Ruth. It will work out. You'll see. He'll be flattered."

So Ruth did.

And Naomi was right. Boaz was flattered out of his mind.

"Oh, Ruth," he said, "thank you for asking me. You honor me. I never thought you'd think of me with all those dashing young men simply crazy about you. I've watched them in the fields, and I've watched you. I'm so glad you didn't want any of them. This really crowns your kindness to Naomi too. I understand all the laws of inheritance, but— oh, let's not get too excited for the moment.

"As our law stands just now, I'm not your nearest kinsman, unfortunately. Some other fellow is a closer relative than I am. He must be given first option to buy the property and to have— you. Oh, I do hope he won't buy. I hope he says no. I'll attend to the matter first thing in the morning.

"My dear, it's very late. You can't go through the streets at this hour. And we mustn't let anyone know that a woman was at the threshing floor all night either. Rest a little while here, and just before everybody gets about in the morning, you go home to Naomi."

So Ruth did as Boaz said. Just as she was setting out in the early morning, he said, "Bring me your shawl." And he poured a bushel and a half of barley onto it, wrapped it round, and put it on her back. "A present for mother-in-law!" he said. His eyes were twinkling and full of love and kindness.

WILLY

Ruth blushed all the way home, as the dawn broke and blushed across the sky that early morning.

Naomi wasn't asleep when Ruth arrived. Very few winks of sleep had Naomi had that night.

"How did you get on, dear? What did he say?"

Ruth told her everything.

"Yes, it's true about that other relative," Naomi said. "But we won't be in suspense for long. Boaz doesn't let the grass grow under his feet. I'm sure he'll see to it first thing this morning.

"Stay indoors, Ruth, and try to be calm and patient. God is in this, I know," Naomi said. "Take a little rest if you can. We'll soon hear what's to happen. We'll know before noon."

6

To Be or Not to Be?

Was Boaz, the most eligible bachelor in Bethlehem, about to be married, or not? There'd been speculations galore from time to time. There are always speculations when there's an eligible bachelor around. People always seem to think he needs a wife. Some people even set about trying to find him one.

There'd been groundless speculations many times before about Boaz, but today nobody knew what was afoot but himself, Naomi, and Ruth.

Boaz was agitated as he strode into the marketplace that morning, looking for the man who stood between him and his heart's desire—an insignificant man until now, but this morning the only man in the world who mattered!

Boaz had been the hearty, honest farmer, heart-whole and happy, the utter despair of the matchmakers—until this lovely young widow had come from Moab with Naomi. That did it!

He'd thought he didn't stand a chance. And then, last night, he had found he did! But—because of the laws about inheritance and kinsmen, someone else had prior claim to her. And Boaz could still lose what, as yet, he'd hardly say he'd gained: Ruth!

It was still early when Boaz reached the marketplace that morning. But many people were about already. The elders were in their places of office in the city gates, ready to settle disputes, sort out problems, and to act as witnesses for the ratification of deals.

Boaz was agitated. To be or not to be?

Ah, there was the insignificant kinsman—the man of the moment this morning.

"Hi! You're the very man I want to see this morning. Got a minute?"

"Sure."

"Good! Well, would you come and sit down here. Little bit o' business this morning. Here, wait a minute. Just let me get some witnesses together."

Boaz quickly asked ten of the head men, elders who were sitting at the city gates, to come and act as witnesses. And they did. They did this kind of thing every day of the week.

As calmly as he could, Boaz began to speak to the kinsman, all the witnesses witnessing:

"You know our relative Naomi—well, actually, it was her husband who was our relative—you know Naomi, who came back to us from Moab at the beginning of harvest time?

67

"Well, she wants to sell our kinsman Elimelech's property. She wants to get the matter settled as soon as possible. I'd like to see the matter settled too. I felt I should speak to you about it so that you can buy the property if you want to—with these worthy elders of the town as witnesses.

"If you want it, let me know right away. Because if you don't buy it, I will. You have first option to buy, but I'm next in line."

"All right," the man said, "I'll buy it."

Boaz's heart sank right down into his sandals. But he hadn't finished talking yet.

Boaz said, "Well, if you buy the land from Naomi, the law of Israel requires that you marry Ruth the Moabitess, and the eldest son of the marriage will carry on her dead husband's name and inherit the property."

"Oh, I couldn't do *that*," the man said. "I couldn't have *her* son becoming heir to my property. That would really mess up the inheritance for my family. You can buy the land."

Did anybody observe Boaz's face at that moment? His heart really missed a beat.

It was a custom in Israel at that time for a man transferring his right of purchase to pull off his sandal and hand it to the other person. This publicly made the deal valid. So, as the man said to Boaz, "You can buy the land," he handed Boaz his sandal.

Then Boaz began to make a speech to the witnesses. And many other townsfolk had gathered round by now to see and hear what was going on.

Boaz, the wealthy farmer and landowner, sitting there holding a sandal, said, "You are all witnesses that today I have bought from Naomi the property that belonged to her late husband, Elimelech, and to her late sons, Mahlon and Chilion. And I do with that purchase take Ruth the Moabitess, Mahlon's widow, to be my wife. Our first son will carry on the family name of her dead husband."

All the people got excited. Women listeners shed tears of joy. "Oh, isn't that lovely? I'm so glad for Ruth. She's a real sweetie. And I'm so glad for Naomi. Won't she be pleased?"

The men shook hands with Boaz; they congratulated him on his good luck. A few of the younger men said, "Did you ever! The lucky old fellow!"

All wished Boaz long life and happiness. "May you be great and successful!" they said. "And may you have many children like your ancestor Judah!"

As soon as it was polite to leave his well-wishers, Boaz headed for Naomi's house. He walked quickly— on air!

His mind was full of Ruth. She'd been brought up a heathen girl in Moab, but her faith in Jehovah now was strong and true.

His own dear mother, Rahab, had been brought up heathen too, but what a follower of Jehovah she was! "And she taught me," Boaz said out loud. "God bless her!"

"Ruth's a wonderful girl, and so very beautiful. Her kindness to Naomi is something out of this world. I'm the luckiest fellow on earth this morning. She'll be waiting in suspense, poor girl, wondering 'to be or not to be.'"

And throwing decorum to the winds, Boaz, the highly respected farmer of Bethlehem, began to run.

And as he burst into Naomi's house with a hearty "God be with you, girls!" he added, "Where's my Ruth?"

Naomi had slipped out into her kitchen to put the finishing touches to the noon meal. Tears were streaming down her face. Tears of joy as she thanked God for His wonderful love and kindness to Ruth—and to herself.

Boaz put his head through the doorway. "Oh, leave that, Naomi. We're going to my house for dinner today. It'll be ready at noon. That's pretty soon. We must be off."

"Oh, that's lovely!" Naomi said. "See you when you return, Ruth."

"What d'you mean, 'See you when you return'?" Boaz said. "You're coming too. We shall need you. We've got plans to make. You must come."

So they went to dinner with Boaz. It was a happy, hilarious meal.

"Well now," Boaz said, "the legal wedding ceremony took place this morning in the marketplace before ten witnesses, and others witnessing. We'll have a great big party to celebrate very soon, and all our friends and townsfolk will come. How about that?"

Well, the news spread round Bethlehem like wildfire. Two ladies met while shopping at the marketplace.

"What d'you know? Boaz is getting married," one greeted the other.

"You don't mean it! Who to?"

"Ruth, Naomi's—"

"Oh, how nice! That's really the nicest thing I've heard. When?"

"The city elders say he is married. They witnessed the ceremony this morning."

"Well," said the first lady, "these older bachelors have the knack of stealing a march on the most observant of us."

No one was left wondering for long, because invitations to the big wedding feast were already on their way to all the townsfolk in Bethlehem. All the grownups were invited, and Boaz insisted that all the children were to come too. Boaz loved kids. There was to be lovely food—and fun for the kids.

And as the preparations began, excitement ran through the town. This was going to be a very popular wedding.

This was going to be the wedding of the year. The wedding of Boaz and Ruth!

7

The Wedding

You never heard such a hum of happy voices as was coming from Boaz's farm that wedding day when the party got into full swing. And above the happy hum you could hear the merry voices of the children playing in the fields. And you could smell the barbecue a mile away.

I just had to get in on it. No, I wasn't gate-crashing the party. As a visitor in Bethlehem, I was most welcome. I didn't want to intrude my presence, though. I wanted to go incognito. So I put on a dress I'd made from material embroidered in Hebron—Hebron's just south of Bethlehem. Other people would be wearing clothes made of the same kind of material, and that was just how I wanted it. In the crowd—the whole town would be there—no one would notice me.

So I made my way down to Boaz's farm and mingled with the crowd—all of them guests at the wedding of Boaz and Ruth.

The bridal party was over there, near the spreading oak trees, mostly hidden at the moment by many people in front of me.

Wait a minute. I could see an old couple there. They looked as if they were important to the occasion. I wondered who they were? Who should I ask?

Right beside me was a friendly, happy sort of man. He was saying "Shalom!" to almost everybody in sight. Just then he turned his head and smiled at me. He nodded and said, "Shalom!" I almost said "Hi!" but instead I said "Shalom!" in my best Hebrew accent.

Then, "Excuse me," I said, "that old couple there who seem to be family, do you know who they are?"

"Oh, yes! They're Boaz's father and mother, Salmon and Rahab, parents of the bridegroom! She's the—"

"Really?" I said. I could hardly believe my luck at seeing them.

"You must be a stranger here not to know them," my informant said.

Then he went on quickly, "Yeah, wonderful people they are. Rahab hid Joshua's two spies. You know all about Joshua? And Salmon? Well, people do say he was one of the spies.

"Wonderful people they are anyway. Salmon was the first to farm this land. One of the early settlers, he was! This is the bit of country that Joshua gave out to the tribe of Judah, and Salmon had land round here. Now Boaz has the farm. I'm givin' you all the fam'ly history! But they're wonderful people, Boaz's mom and dad— Salmon and Rahab."

Just then they moved, and I got a better view of them.

"I can well believe it," I said.

This chap knows a thing or two, I said to myself. *I'll keep tabs on him and ask him anything else I want to know.*

"I was looking for Naomi," I said. "I can't see her anywhere."

"She's right there," my companion said. "That's her, dressed in blue, talkin' to the broad-shouldered man with his back to us. That's the bridegroom, by the way."

"Oh," I said, but I was gazing at the happy, white-haired lady in blue. "No!" I said, "that can't be Naomi."

"Oh, yes, 'tis," he said. "That's her all right. She looks so happy and young that you don't know her. But that's Naomi. A wonderful woman! She's been through so much trouble. Lost her husband and two boys—all she'd got—one after the other, just like that. But she's risen above it all. Strong faith in Jehovah. That's it. It's a wonderful day for her!"

Evidently the bridegroom was teasing her now. And she was teasing him back. Ah, now the bridegroom, Boaz, turned to face my way. I'm sure his bride was there somewhere beside him, but at the moment, people's heads blocked my view.

"Boaz looks handsome and happy," I said, "as if he's found a million dollars."

"He's found something better than that," my informant said. "He's found a good wife. And her price is far above rubies! Just look at her!"

Someone in front of me moved. Then I saw her! A beautiful young woman with a sweet, shy expression on her face. Her dark eyes twinkled and shone with joy. She looked lovely in her simple wedding dress. A lovely, lovely lady.

"Ain't she beautiful? And her character's the same. Why, I remember the first day I saw her. She came to ask if she could glean."

"What do you mean, 'glean'?" I asked.

"Well, in Israel poor people and widows can come into the harvest fields and pick up the grain that the reapers have missed and keep it for food.

"Ruth came to ask me if she could glean in my boss's field. Boaz is my boss. I'm his farm manager—and proud of it."

"When Ruth came, I could see everything was strange to her. She told me who she was. She'd come from Moab with Naomi."

"I'd heard of her. All the town had. Those words Ruth had said to Naomi was talked of by everybody."

"Naomi had told all her friends, of course, 'cause those words had meant everything to her when Ruth said 'em. 'I'll never leave you,' Ruth said. 'Your people shall be my people, and your God shall be my God.' So she left her heathen gods and came to Jehovah.

"And look! God has blessed the whole lot of 'em because of Ruth. My boss was taken with her right from the start. Of course, she is lovely. But he kept telling us fellows on the farm, 'Be kind to her. She's left her own home to come here to follow Jehovah!' He said God would bless her for it."

Just then a shout went up. "God bless you, sir—and your lady!"

"That's Boaz's farm boys," my companion told me. "They love him. They're a merry lot."

"God be with you, boys!" Boaz said in his cheery voice. "Enjoying the party?"

Then Boaz, the bridegroom, made an announce-
ment.

"Come, friends! Time to eat! Sit down, all of you."

And we all sat down to a sumptuous, happy feast.

Barbecue fires had been lit, and loaded spits had been turning and sizzling since before dawn. Bakers and pastry cooks had delivered stacks of tempting goodies. Huge bowls of luscious fruit—just waiting to be eaten—and great, cool stone jars stood about full of delicious drinks. The feast lasted a long time. Just so many good things to eat!

Well, as usual the boys and girls were up and off to play as soon as they'd eaten their fill. Their merry voices rang out in Boaz's meadow, like recess at our school!

The grownups sat around awhile to talk and reminisce. Then we all joined together again for fun and games.

The party went on and on. No one wanted it to stop. But eventually, late—or early—we all went to rest, caught up in the joy of the occasion, wrapped round with friendship and loving kindness.

Actually, the celebrating was to go on for about a week. So we'd be back tomorrow. And the next day. Just imagine the fun and friendship—at the wedding of the year.

Boaz and Ruth set up house. Knowing Boaz and Ruth, you'd expect them to have a happy home. Well, they did.

Generous people! They wouldn't hear of Naomi living anywhere but with them. Their house was big. Naomi could have her own rooms there. And her friends could come and visit. They did.

It wasn't long before there was great excitement. Naomi told everybody. She just couldn't help it. She was so excited. She was going to be a grandmother! Of course, it was Ruth who was going to have the baby!

God was so good to Ruth and Boaz (and Naomi), and He gave them a little son.

How Naomi loved that baby! She hugged him. And bathed him. And took him for walks. And made him clothes. And helped Ruth get his food ready. Naomi was busy with that baby—of course, she was a built-in baby-sitter.

You'd have thought the baby was hers. Well, in a way, he was. He was to carry on the family name of Elimelech and Mahlon. You remember about "redeeming the inheritance"?

Ruth didn't mind at all. She was glad to have Grandma Naomi's help with her first baby.

Dear me! I haven't told you the baby's name. Well, of course, all three of them discussed it—Boaz, Ruth, and Naomi—with the help of friends! And they came up with Obed. But nobody except God knew what an important baby this was.

The last picture we have of Naomi in the Bible is a happy one: she is holding baby Obed on her lap, and her old friends are dropping in to visit and see the new baby—as friends will do with their baby gifts. And they are all congratulating Naomi on her lovely grandchild.

WILLY

"He'll take care of you when you're old," one friend said as she looked at the baby. "He'll take after his dear, kind mother, Ruth, who's been kinder to you already than seven sons could have been."

Obed grew up to be a fine man. And when he married, he had a fine son, whose name was Jesse. And Jesse was the father of the great King David.

So we're back where we started at the beginning of this book, with King David's family tree.

8

All in God's Plan

King David's family tree is in the Book of Ruth in the Bible, along with the story I've told you. You can find it. (Actually, the family tree starts way back with one of Jacob's sons, Judah—Joseph's brother.)

Ruth, the Moabitess, was King David's great-grandmother.

Also, did you know that Rahab, King David's great-great-grandmother (Boaz's mother), is given honorable mention for faith in God's Honor List in Hebrews, chapter 11, in the Bible?

I do like the people in King David's family tree, don't you? Especially Ruth and Boaz.

Oh, but wait a minute. There's one more exciting thing about these people. They are also in the family tree of our Lord Jesus Christ, because King David was His earthly ancestor. You can read all of their names in the Christmas story in Matthew, chapter 1, in the Bible.

When Ruth clung to Naomi that day on the side of the road leading to Bethlehem, saying as she did so, "Your God shall be my God," she had no idea that she was stepping into a very important place in God's great plan.

And as Ruth lived her brave, quiet life, along with the rest of the people in our story who lived their brave, quiet lives with all their joys and sorrows, she didn't know, and they didn't know, that their names would become immortal.

It never occurred to them that their names were going down in the genealogy—the family tree—of great King David, the greatest king of Israel. And in the family tree of great King David's greater Son, Jesus Christ, the King of Kings himself!

Be sure to look for the other books in Mrs. G.'s *Come, Meet* series.